All apples are green at first.

Not all ripe apples are red.

Golden Delicious apples are yellow.

ed Delicious, McIntosh, nd Fuji are red apples.

Granny Smith apples are green.

An apple tree can grow to be about 7 times as tall as a person.

Dwarf apple trees are short, so their apples are easy to pick.

Things apples make: pies, cakes, apple butter, turnovers, applesauce, juice, caramel apples, and more.

Johnny Appleseed planted thousands of apple trees for American pioneers.

Some apple trees are over 100 years old.

Washingto... apples than any other state in the United States.

Apple Countdown

Joan Holub   Illustrated by Jan Smith

Albert Whitman & Company, Morton Grove, Illinois

For Kristen Shaheen, a good apple.—J.H.

To my dad, George Smith,
whom I couldn't manage without!—J.S.

Library of Congress Cataloging-in-Publication Data

Holub, Joan.
Apple countdown / by Joan Holub ; illustrated by Jan Smith.
p. cm.
Summary: Rhyming text describes a school field trip to an apple orchard, where the students count down all the things
they see, from twenty nametags to one apple pie.
ISBN 978-0-8075-0398-0
[1. Stories in rhyme. 2. School field trips—Fiction. 3. Orchards—Fiction. 4. Counting.] I. Smith, Jan, ill. II. Title.
PZ8.3.H74Ap 2009 [E]—dc22 2008031705

The design is by Carol Gildar.

For more information about Albert Whitman,
please visit our web site at www.albertwhitman.com.

"Field trip day! Hooray!" says José.

"**Twenty** apples with our names," says James.

"I see a tag for me," says Lee.

"**Nineteen** kids get on our bus," says Russ.

"I share with Mr. Yee," says Lee.

"**Eighteen** miles till we're there," says Claire.

"Eight miles, turn, then go ten," says Ben.

"Name **seventeen** things we might see," says Mr. Yee.

"An apple tree!" calls Lee.

"**Sixteen** steps to the gate," says Kate.

"Hi, Farmer Applebee," says Lee.

"**Fifteen** cars on a train," says Elaine.

"Five yellow. Five green. Five red," says Ted.

"**Fourteen** cows. Moo! Moo!" says Sue.
"That's twelve cows plus two."

"**Thirteen** ducks. Quack! Quack!" says Zack.
"Ten white ones and three black."

Red Delicious

Granny Smith

"**Twelve** rows of trees," says Louise.

"And **eleven** hives for bees."

"Yay! It's time to pick!" says Nick.

1. Hold apple in your hand, pressing the stem against the apple with your index finger.
2. Twist upward.
3. Pull gently.

Lee

"Easy as one, two, three," says Lee.

"I picked small ones!
My sack will hold **ten**," says Ben.

"I picked bigger ones," says Caroline.
"My sack will hold **nine**."

"Mine are the biggest!"
says Kate.
"My sack holds only **eight**!"

"My **seven** apples are green," says Christine.
"My **six** apples are red," says Ted.
"Want to trade with me?" asks Lee.

"An apple has **five** holes, each with seeds inside," says Clyde.

"There are **four** seasons in a year," says Shakir.

"Winter branches are bare," says Claire.

"Spring flowers bloom, pink and white," says Dwight.

"In summer the apples grow," says Jo.

"Fall apples are ready to pick," says Nick.

"**Three** apple pies for us!" says Russ.
"How many slices are there?" asks Claire.
"Two times six, plus eight," says Kate.

"**TWO** o'clock. Time to go," says Jo.

"Crunch Crunch Crunch Crunch . . .

CRUNCH!"
"**One** lost tooth . . . for me!" shouts Lee.

APPLE FACTS

There is a five-pointed star shape inside every apple.

Apples float because they are 25% air.

An apple has 5-10 seeds inside.

Apples are good for you! They contain vitamins A and C and potassium.

The most popular apple in the United States is Red Delicious

There are over 2,500 kinds of apples in the United States.

There are over 7,500 kinds of apples grown in the world.

New kinds of apples are discovered every year.

Apple blossoms are pink, but they turn white.

An apple blossom has five petals.

Without bees to pollinate apple blossoms, trees could not grow apples.